HAVE YOU THANKED AN INVENTOR TODAY?

BY
PATRICE
McLAURIN

Have You Thanked An Inventor Today? by Patrice McLaurin

Books may be purchased in quantity and/or special sales by emailing info@hytait.com.

Published by: Digital Arts Publishing, LLC. Lawrenceville, GA
Illustrated by: Dian Wang
Creative Consultant: Darren McLaurin

ISBN: 978-0-9973152-0-2
10 9 8 7 6 5 4 3 2 1
1. Children's 2. Picture 3. African-American 4. Poetry
Second Edition
Printed in United States

digital arts publishing

This world is full of inventions,

some of them we don't even think about.

But if we took the time to think about them,

we'd realize we wouldn't want to live without them.

You see, inventions, they make our lives much easier, and they also make our lives more fun! So we should thank the inventors, who invent great inventions, for without them, we might not get anything done!

Like, for instance, when your mom wakes you up in the morning, to let you know that it's time to go to school. You stretch and yawn, rub the corners of your eyes and probably wipe away last night's drool!

THANK YOU!

BenjaminBanneker

That's when you happen to glance over at your clock, and realize that you're running a bit late; well you wouldn't know that were it not for Benjamin Banneker, he invented the first clock in the United States!

So you put on clothes and you rush into the bathroom!
You wash your face and brush your teeth, then brush your
hair. Well you should thank Lyda Newman, for part of your
morning groomin', as the modern day hair brush,
was her awesome idea!

THANK YOU!
Lyda Newman

THANK YOU!

John Standard

Afterwards, you're called into the kitchen
for breakfast. This morning it's cereal
with fruit and wheat toast.
Well thank goodness John Standard
improved the refrigerator,
because hot milk with your cereal is pretty gross!

And when you're on your way to school,
whether you're a bus rider, a car rider or you walk;
you have to thank Garrett Morgan for the traffic light,
otherwise none of our streets would be safe to cross!

8

Then, after you've settled into your classroom, and you've taken out your supplies because **you're such a scholar**; please remember to show love to Mr. John Love, for his invention was none other than the pencil sharpener!

THANK YOU!

John Love

Now, as much as I know that you love to learn,
you'll admit that sometimes, lunch is your favorite
time of day. Well you can thank John Robinson for
your lunchbox, but for what's inside it, it's your mom
that you need to thank.

THANK YOU!

John Robinson

And what does mom usually pack in your lunchbox?

Tasty snacks that make your belly go yum!

Like peanut butter, made popular by George Washington Carver,

or potato chips, invented by George Crum!

THANK YOU!
GeorgeWashingtonCarver

THANK YOU!
George Crum

Fast forward, the school day is now over. It's been a long one, and you're happy to be home. You check the mailbox invented by P. Downing,

THANK YOU!
P. Downing

then chill in front of the air conditioner invented by Frederick Jones. **

THANK YOU!
Frederick Jones

**See Biography for update

Plus your teacher didn't assign any homework,
so you decide to play a few games on the cell phone.
Well if it wasn't for Henry Sampson's gamma electric cell,
believe it or not, there would be no cell phone!

THANK YOU!

Henry Sampson

And these are just a few awesome inventions!

There are countless other ones that I didn't even mention!

Like the doorknob invented by O. Dorsey,

or a type of guitar invented by Robert Fleming!

Sarah Boone invented the ironing board
and Thomas Steward invented the mop!
Lonnie Johnson invented the super soaker
and W.A. Martin, he improved the lock!

So now, here's what I want you to do,
I'd like for you to take a moment or two;
and ponder over how life would be
if these inventions weren't created for you.

THEN DREAM ABOUT WHAT YOU'D LIKE TO INVENT!

Biographies

Benjamin Banneker was a mathematician, astronomer and writer. He invented America's first clock in the early 1750's, and he helped to design the city of Washington D.C.! Thank you Benjamin Banneker!

**Frederick McKinley Jones was a mechanical and electrical engineer. Though his patent states that he invented an air conditioning unit, Jones actually invented the first automatic refrigeration system for trucks; thus revolutionizing the grocery business! The air conditioner was invented by Willis Carrier. Thank you Frederick Jones!

Garrett Morgan was a repairman and business owner. He invented the three light traffic signal in 1923. He also invented an improved sewing machine and the gas mask. Thank you Garrett Morgan!

George Washington Carver was a teacher at the Tuskegee Institute. He invented over 100 products with the peanut and the sweet potato. Thank you George Washington Carver!

Biographies

George Crum was a cook and a restaurant owner. He invented the potato chip in 1853. Thank you George Crum!

Henry Thomas Sampson, Jr. is an inventor and a nuclear engineer. He invented the gamma-electric cell, which is the cell used in powering cell phones, in 1971. Thank you Henry Thomas Sampson, Jr.!

John Lee Love was an inventor. He invented the portable pencil sharpener in 1889. This pencil sharpener was also known as the "Love Sharpener". Thank you John Love!

John Robinson was an inventor. He invented the lunchbox in the 1890's. Thank you John Robinson!

Biographies

John Standard was an inventor. He invented an improved model of the refrigerator in 1891. He also invented an improved oil stove. Thank you John Standard!

Lonnie G. Johnson is a nuclear engineer. He invented the super soaker water gun in 1982. He also worked on space missions to Jupiter and Saturn. Thank you Lonnie G. Johnson!

Lyda Newman was a hairdresser and a women's rights activist. She invented an improved model of the hairbrush in 1898. She also fought for women's right to vote. Thank you Lyda Newman!

Osbourn Dorsey was an inventor. He invented the doorknob in 1878. He also invented the doorstop. Thank you O. Dorsey!

Biographies

 P. B. Downing was an inventor. He invented the street letter mailbox in 1891. He also invented an electrical switch for railroads. Thank you Philip B. Downing!

Robert Flemming Jr. was an inventor. He is best known for inventing a version of the guitar in 1886. Thank you Robert Flemming Jr.!

Sarah Boone was an inventor. She invented the ironing board in 1892. Thank you Sarah Boone!

Thomas Stewart was an inventor. He invented an improved version of the mop in 1893. He also invented a metal bending machine. Thank you Thomas Stewart!

W. A. Martin, was an inventor. He invented an improved version of the lock in 1889. Thank you W.A. Martin.!

WHAT AM I?

Have fun solving the riddles below!

1. If you walk into a room and you find that it's really hot, you can turn me on and I'll cool it down a lot! What am I? (Air Conditioner)

2. I keep milk from spoiling and I keep veggies fresh. I guess you can say, that I help food, to taste its very best. What am I? (Refrigerator)

3. People love me because I help traffic to flow. My red means stop and my green means go. What am I? (Traffic Light)

4. I have two hands, yet I don't have any arms. People often use me if they need an alarm. What am I? (Clock)

5. I am the perfect place to keep your snacks. You can place me in your cubby and in your backpack. What am I? (Lunchbox)

WHAT AM I?

6. I'm often filled with letters, but they're not the alphabet. It's always nice to open me and find a letter from a friend. What am I? (Mailbox)

7. You can play with my strings, but you can't tie them in knots. People sometimes use me when they're ready to rock! What am I? (Guitar)

8. My bristles may be hard, but they help me to look smooth. Mom often makes me use this before I go to school. What am I? (Hair Brush)

9. I help the pencil to remain sharp so that it can help you to remain smart. What am I? (Pencil Sharpener)

10. If there's a huge spill you'll be happy that I'm around. I usually clean up messes that are on the floor or on the ground. What am I? (Mop or Broom)

WHAT AM I?

Directions: Circle the correct answers to the questions below.

1. You can use me to cool down your home if it's really hot. What am I?

    a. an air conditioner

    b. a CD player

    c. a radio

2. You can put orange juice in me to keep it cool. What am I?

    n. a refrigerator

    o. a TV

    p. a chair

3. I am used to help traffic flow smoothly. What am I?

    g. a lamp

    h. a bicycle

    i. a traffic light

4. People sometimes use me when they need an alarm to wake up in the morning. What am I?

    m. a stove

    n. a clock

    o. a light bulb

5. I am the perfect place to keep your lunch. What am I?

    t. a pencil

    u. a piano

    v. a lunchbox

6. If you receive a letter from grandma, the postman will place it inside of me.

   What am I?

   d.   a dishwasher

   e.   a mailbox

   f.   a closet

7. I make awesome music, the kind that makes you rock. What am I?

   n.   a guitar

   o.   a bar of soap

   p.   a computer

8. I can be used to make your hair look nice. What am I?

   r.   a bed

   s.   an umbrella

   t.   a hair brush

9. When your pencil gets dull, I help to make it sharp again. What am I?

   n. a can opener

   o.   a pencil sharpener

   p.   a cell phone

10. You can use me to help to clean up spills. What am I?

   p.   a lock

   q.   a comb

   r.   a mop

Place the letter of the correct answers on the lines below.

WHAT AM I?

____ ____ ____ ____ ____ ____ ____ ____ ____ ____!

1   2   3   4   5   6   7   8   9   10

INVENTION BOX

MATERIALS NEEDED:

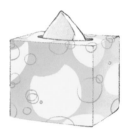

A Cube Tissue Box

Construction Paper

Tape

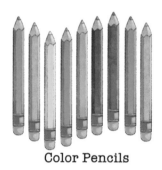

Color Pencils

INSTRUCTIONS:

This activity encourages creativity. Choose an inventor from the book.
Using the cube tissue box, cover it with construction paper
(keep the opening at the bottom). On side one write the name of the
inventor and tell a little bit about him/her. On side two, write the
name of the invention and draw picture of it. On side 3, tell how life
is much easier/better/safer because of the invention. On side four, tell
what life might be like without the invention. You can then use the
boxes as room decorations, classroom tissue boxes, hallway
displays, etc..

WHAT WOULD YOU LIKE TO INVENT?
(Group Project)

DIRECTIONS: Using your imagination,
brainstorm with your group and think of
an invention that would make life easier,
safer, or more fun.

After you determine your invention, answer the questions below.

What is the name of your invention?_____

What does your invention do?_____

_____

_____

_____

How will your invention make life easier, safer or more fun? _____

_____

_____

_____

About the Author

Patrice McLaurin has worked to empower and to enhance the
lives of young people for well over 15 years. Her journey began
as a volunteer at a local Girls Inc., where she taught a cultural
heritage course, designed to promote self-esteem and
self-determination. From there, she coordinated and facilitated
numerous youth workshops. As a character education
coordinator, she traveled to various school systems and implemented character
education curriculum; while conjointly working with young women at a girl's
detention center. She's also worked with youth at local alternative schools.

Have You Thanked an Inventor Today?© is Patrice's first children's book.
Her goal is to demonstrate to children, how the genius of African-American mind
is utilized on a daily basis. She also hopes to inspire children to recognize their
own genius. Patrice McLaurin is a native of Bessemer, AL and a graduate of
Alabama A&M University. She currently resides in Lawrenceville, GA with her
husband and two children.

pmclaurin@hytait.com
facebook.com/thankaninventor
instagram.com/patricemclaurin
twitter.com/mclaurinwrites
www.hytait.com

Sources

Benjamin Banneker

"Benjamin Banneker." Notable Black American Men, Book II, edited by Jessie Carney Smith, Gale, 1998. Biography In Context, https://bit.ly/2POnKp4. Accessed 24 Aug. 2018.

Bedini, Silvio A. "Banneker, Benjamin." Encyclopedia of African-American Culture and History, edited by Colin A. Palmer, 2nd ed., vol. 1, Macmillan Reference USA, 2006, pp. 186-188. GVRL.blackhistorymonth, https://bit.ly/2O17ZxM. Accessed 24 Aug. 2018.

Sarah Boone

Boone, S. Ironing Board No. 473,653, United States Patent and Trademark Office, 26 April 1892. USPTO Patent Full-Text and Image Database, https://bit.ly/2xBcchF

Biography.com Editors, "Sarah Boon Biography", Biography.com, A&E Television Networks, 26 August 2018, https://bit.ly/2MSQ33M

Brodie, James Michael, Created Equal: The Lives and Ideas of Black American Innovators. New York: Bill Adler Books, 1993. Print

George Washington Carver

"Who Invented Peanut Butter?." National Peanut Board, 2018, https://bit.ly/2M9Jj5m. Accessed 24 Aug. 2018.

"Culture and Change: Black History in America." Scholastic.com, https://bit.ly/2OI5rBS

George Crum

"George Crum." Gale Biography in Context, Gale, 2009. Biography In Context, https://bit.ly/2MQKO4w. Accessed 24 Aug. 2018.

"George Crum." Gale Biography in Context, Gale, 2017. Biography In Context, https://bit.ly/2QNeYsQ. Accessed 24 Aug. 2018.

"George Crum." Contemporary Black Biography, vol. 101, Gale, 2012. Biography In Context, https://bit.ly/2QKvyJL. Accessed 24 Aug. 2018.

O. Dorsey

Dorsey, O. Door Holding Device No. 210,764, United States Patent and Trademark Office, 10 December 1878. USPTO Patent Full-Text and Image Database, https://bit.ly/2Di25Eu

"Who Is O. Dorsey?". Reference.com, IAC Publishing, https://bit.ly/2po8ofI. Accessed 24 Aug 2018

Egan, James. The Mega Misconception Book. Lulu Publishing 2016. Print

Philip Downing

Webster, Raymond B. "Philip B. Downing." African American Firsts in Science & Technology, Gale, 1999. Biography In Context, https://bit.ly/2xrhkp1. Accessed 24 Aug. 2018.

Downing, P.B. Street Letter Box. No. 462,092, United States Patent and Trademark Office, 27 October 1891. USPTO Patent Full-Text and Image Database, https://bit.ly/2ppHVOY

Robert F. Fleming, Jr.

Fleming, R.F. Guitar No. 338,727, United States Patent and Trademark Office, 30 March 1886. USPTO Patent Full-Text and Image Database, https://bit.ly/2OKz5Xm

"Who Was Black Inventor Robert Fleming, Jr.?". Reference.com, IAC Publishing, https://bit.ly/2xtDw29. Accessed 24 Aug 2018

Lonnie Johnson

"Lonnie G. Johnson." Contemporary Black Biography, vol. 93, Gale, 2011. Biography In Context, https://bit.ly/2MQGsKJ. Accessed 24 Aug. 2018.

Adams, Susan. "The Inventor Of The Super Soaker Talks About Turning Inventions Into Products And His Next Big Idea". Forbes.com, Forbes Magazine, 3 March 2017. https://bit.ly/2OFrxVz

Snyder, Chris and Stuart, Matthew. "Meet the man who invented the Super Soaker — one of the best-selling toys of all time". BusinessInsider.com, Insider Inc, 17 August 2017. https://read.bi/2xrGSm6

Frederick Jones

Biography.com Editors, "Frederick Jones Biography", Biography.com, A&E Television Networks, https://bit.ly/2EbCOMf. Accessed 24 Aug. 2018.

Jones, F.M. Air Conditioning Unit. Des 132,182, United States Patent and Trademark Office, 28 April 1942. USPTO Patent Full-Text and Image Database, https://bit.ly/2DjOheg

"Willis Haviland Carrier." Merriam Webster's Biographical Dictionary, Merriam-Webster, 1995. Biography In Context, https://bit.ly/2PTOOjA. Accessed 24 Aug. 2018.

Sources

John Love

Love, J.L. Pencil Sharpener. No. 594,114, United States Patent and Trademark Office, 23 November 1897. USPTO Patent Full-Text and Image Database, https://bit.ly/2NXMvBT

Webster, Raymond B. "John Lee Love." African American Firsts in Science & Technology, Gale, 1999. Biography In Context, https://bit.ly/2NpidbM. Accessed 24 Aug. 2018.

Momon, Matthew T. Africa: It's True Role in the Ancient World: An Informal Analysis: Xlibris Corporation, 2012. Print.

W.A. Martin

Martin, W.A. Lock. No. 407,738, United States Patent and Trademark Office, 23 July 1889. USPTO Patent Full-Text and Image Database, https://bit.ly/2MQvSU1

"This Week in Black History". Jet Magazine July 1999: 19 Print.

Garrett Morgan

"Garrett Morgan." Contemporary Black Biography, vol. 1, Gale, 1992. Biography In Context, https://bit.ly/2O1yd36. Accessed 24 Aug. 2018.

Morgan, Garrett. Three Way Traffic Signal. No. 1,475,024, United States Patent and Trademark Office, 20 November 1923. https://bit.ly/2AY0Ynm

Lyda Newman

Newman, L.D. Brush. No. 614,335, United States Patent and Trademark Office, 15 November 1898. USPTO Patent Full-Text and Image Database, https://bit.ly/2MQGH8T

Biography.com Editors, "Lyda Newman Birography" Biography.com, A&E Television Networks, 2 April 2014, https://bit.ly/2Nrnz6p

" Profile: Lyda D. Newman" BlackElephants.com, 21 February 2014, https://bit.ly/2PVo85r

John Robinson

Wilson, Donald and Wilson, Jane Y. The Pride of African American History: Inventors, Scientists, Physicians. Authorhouse Publishing, 2003. Print

Butler, John, Sibley. Entrepreneurship and Self-Help Among Black Americans. SUNY Press, 2005. Print.

Robinson, J. Dinner Pail. No. 356,852 United States Patent and Trademark Office, 1 February 1887. USPTO Patent Full-Text and Image Database, https://bit.ly/2poZGxN

John Standard

Webster, Raymond B. "J. Standard." African American Firsts in Science & Technology, Gale, 1999. Biography In Context, https://bit.ly/2prMKXW. Accessed 24 Aug. 2018.

Standard, J. Refrigerator. No. 455,981, United States Patent and Trademark Office, 14 July 1891. USPTO Patent Full-Text and Image Database, https://bit.ly/2PPFO2b

Momon, Matthew T. Africa: It's True Role in the Ancient World: An Informal Analysis: Xlibris Corporation, 2012. Print.

Henry Sampson

Webster, Raymond B. "Henry T. Sampson." African American Firsts in Science & Technology, Gale, 1999. Biography In Context, https://bit.ly/2QNgkDW. Accessed 24 Aug. 2018.

Sampson, Henry. Gamma Electric Cell. No. 3,591,860, United States Patent and Trademark Office, 6 July 1971. USPTO Patent Full Text and Image Database, https://bit.ly/2OFLICU

CBM Newswire, "Dr. Henry T. Sampson, Jr. Gamma Electric Cell Remembered". Sacobserver.com, Sacramento Observer, 8 July 2015. https://bit.ly/2MQM9IA

Tom Stewart

Stewart, T.W. Mop. No. 499,402, United States Patent and Trademark Office, 13 June 1893. USPTO Patent Full-Text and Image Database, https://bit.ly/2PRjllu

MacIntyre, John, Amazing Mom Book. Naperville: Sourcebooks, 2005. Print.

Bellis, Mary, "Thomas Stewart – Mop", theinventors.org, The New York Times Company, 2006, https://bit.ly/2Dejpdo

CPSIA information can be obtained
at www.ICGtesting.com
Printed in the USA
LVRC020758240920
666947LV00007B/15

* 9 7 8 0 9 9 7 3 1 5 2 3 3 *